One Hundred Monkeys

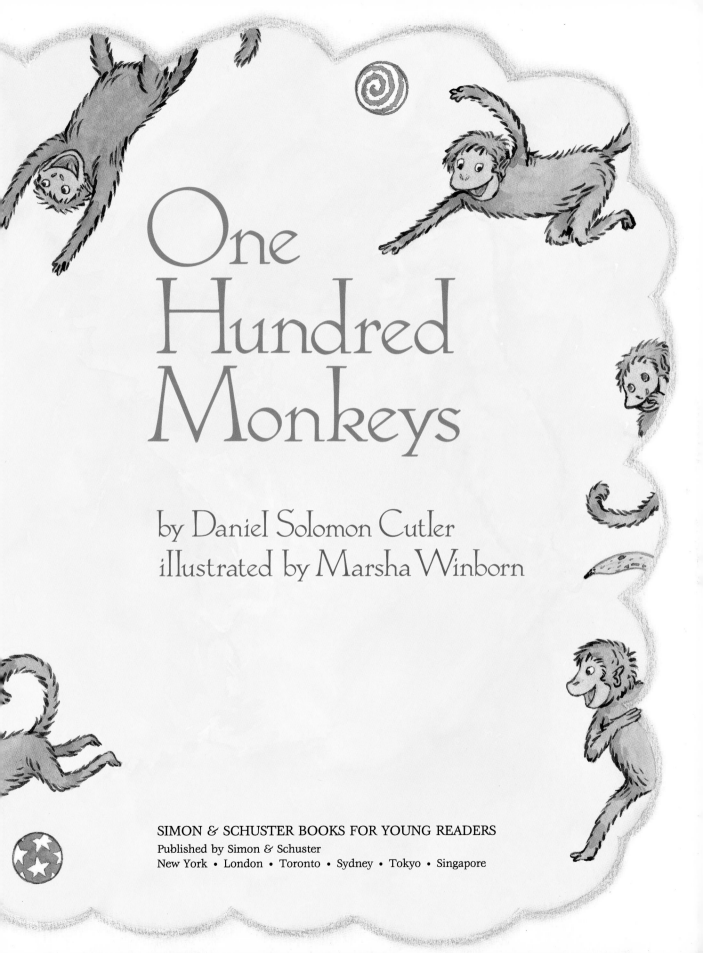

One Hundred Monkeys

by Daniel Solomon Cutler

illustrated by Marsha Winborn

SIMON & SCHUSTER BOOKS FOR YOUNG READERS

Published by Simon & Schuster

New York • London • Toronto • Sydney • Tokyo • Singapore

SIMON & SCHUSTER BOOKS FOR YOUNG READERS
Simon & Schuster Building, Rockefeller Center
1230 Avenue of the Americas, New York, New York 10020

SIMON & SCHUSTER BOOKS FOR YOUNG READERS
is a trademark of Simon & Schuster.

The text for this book is set in 14 pt. Veljovic Book.
The display type is Locarno Light.
The illustrations were done in watercolor and pastel.

Designed by Vicki Kalajian
Manufactured in Hong Kong

10   9   8   7   6   5   4   3   2   1

Library of Congress Cataloging-in-Publication Data
Cutler, Daniel S.   One hundred monkeys /
by Daniel S. Cutler; illustrated by Marsha Winborn.
p.   cm.   Summary: A young boy describes his adventures
with the one hundred monkeys that live near his house.
[1. Monkeys—Fiction.   2. Play—Fiction.]   I. Winborn,
Marsha, ill.   II. Title.   PZ7.C9770n   1991   [E]—dc20   90-22446
ISBN 0-671-73564-0

For Naomi
—D.S.C.

To my own sweet,
funny little monkey
—M.W.

One hundred monkeys live in a house
on the corner of the street two blocks over. from my house

They don't go to my school. They go to a special school for monkeys, where they learn all the rules that monkeys live by in the jungle.

My mother doesn't like me to play with them because
they can be so wild. I come home and I'm wild, too.

Then my mother says, "You are overstimulated" or "You are really wound up. You had better start calming down right now, young man!" (When she's mad, she sometimes calls me "young man" even though I'm just a boy.)

One time, when I was coming home from school, I walked past the monkeys' house. All one hundred of them were playing in their front yard. They asked me if I wanted to play with them. I did....I wanted to play with them very much. So I followed them down into their basement.

We had so much fun playing in their basement that
I didn't notice how late it was until their mother called
down the stairs, "It's time for supper, you little monkeys."

Suppertime already? It must be very late!
I should have called my mother and told her where
I was, but I was afraid she would make me come home.
I was having too much fun. I decided to go home right
after I ate dinner with the monkeys.

We all went upstairs together. I don't think their
parents even noticed me.

We had bananas for dinner.
We ate them in a tree. It was fun! After dinner,
the monkeys' father said to their mother,
"Dear, these little monkeys have been very good.
What do you say we all go out for a treat after
we've done the dishes?"

"An excellent idea," the mother monkey said.
The one hundred monkeys got very excited and
started jabbering all at once. My mother would
have told me to calm down, but the monkey
parents said, "No treats for you children unless
you jabber louder and act a lot more wild!"

We all went outside and got into the monkeys' car. The parents sat in the front with the littlest monkey fastened into a car seat between them. The rest of us squeezed into the back.

We were driving along when—BANG!—we had a flat tire. "Ooh, I hate cars!" the father monkey said. "They're never anything but trouble. Take to the trees!"

The one hundred monkeys scrambled out of the car and climbed the trees. I did, too. We went swinging through the branches, over the houses, and over the cars and over people's heads. The littlest monkey held on to its mother. I was even better at swinging than the monkeys.

We raced to the ice cream store and I got there first.
We all ordered banana splits without any ice cream.

*of course—
no*

When we got home it was time to go to sleep. First we
put on our pajamas. Then we jumped on the beds until
one by one the monkeys settled down and closed their
eyes. I was still jumping after everyone else had fallen
asleep.

Finally I snuggled under the covers, too, smiling to
myself. I liked this monkey business.

The next morning I got up and went to school with the hundred monkeys. We learned songs and special dances that they do in the jungle.

This is a dance they do when monkeys in the jungle get married.

This is a dance monkeys do on Monkey New Year.

This is what they do when they get ready to fight.

Suddenly the teacher turned to me with a frown on her face. She looked very mean. "Where is your tail!" she demanded.

"Do you mean that silly long **thing** that hangs down in
the back?...It broke off in the **bathtub**," I answered.

All the little monkeys laugh**ed**. It made me feel quite
proud that I could make them laugh. They must like me.

"Young man, we don't like smart-mouthed students in
this school," the teacher said. "**You are** going to have to
go into Time Out."

The little monkeys began to wail and cry. "Please, Madame, don't put him into Time Out. He'll be good. We promise." It made me feel good to hear my friends sticking up for me.

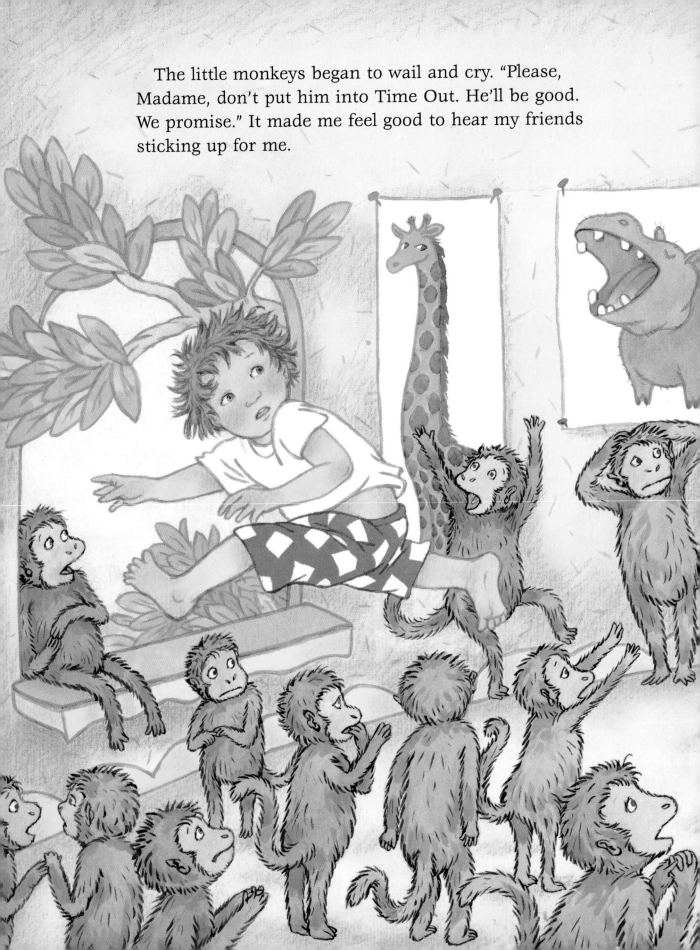

But the mean teacher paid no attention. She called in some big apes to take me into Time Out. I took one look at them and jumped right out of the window!

I was running along the telephone wires like a monkey
when I heard my mother's voice coming through the line.
She was talking on the telephone to my grandmother.

"I'm so sad and worried," she was saying. "That little
rascal still hasn't come home yet."

"Bake something good that he likes," Grandma said.
"That will bring him home."

"Yeah," I said into the wire, using my best "grandmother voice." "Bake him some chocolate chip cookies and one hundred pies and let him eat them whenever he wants. And tell him he doesn't have to go to bed ever again."

"Okay, Mother, if you think that's what's best," my mother answered. "I'll start baking right away."

I laughed so hard I fell off the wire. But I wasn't afraid.
I knew I could fly! It was easy—like swimming in the air.
I flew all the way to my own house—right through my
parents' bedroom window.

I landed on their bed, jumped to the floor, and walked into the bathroom to wash my face and hands.

After I was finished, I walked downstairs. My mother was in the kitchen, baking. She looked up at me and said, "There you are!"

A plate of fresh chocolate chip cookies sat on the table. I started eating them. Before I was finished, my mother pulled a pie from the oven. She put it on the table in front of me, and I took a piece of that, too.

She didn't even tell me to wait until it cooled down. I guess she really must have missed me!